Venturing Beyond Earth
Jesus and the Search for Extraterrestrial Life

Table of Contents

1. Introduction 1
2. The Fusion of Faith and Science 2
   - 2.1. Understanding The Cosmos Through Science 2
   - 2.2. Unfolding Jesus' Teachings 3
   - 2.3. The Confluence of Faith and Science 3
   - 2.4. Archway To Harmony 4
3. Jesus's Teachings: A New Interpretation 6
   - 3.1. Jesus's Teachings and the Universe 6
   - 3.2. The Kingdom of God: An Expanded View 7
   - 3.3. Jesus and Our Cosmic Neighbors 7
   - 3.4. Concluding Thoughts 7
4. The Understanding of Life Beyond Earth 9
   - 4.1. Jesus: The Extraterrestrial Life and Christianity 9
   - 4.2. Exploring the Unknown: Science at the Frontier 10
   - 4.3. The Confluence: Where Spiritual Quest Meets Scientific Venture 10
   - 4.4. Working Hypotheses and Theology 11
   - 4.5. Ethical Considerations on Extraterrestrial Life 11
   - 4.6. Conclusion: A Conscious Leap Into the Vast Cosmos 11
5. Christianity in the Era of Astronomical Discoveries 13
   - 5.1. The Astronomical Pursuit in the Middle Ages 13
   - 5.2. Towards Enlightened Horizons 14
   - 5.3. Design in the Great Clockwork Universe 14
   - 5.4. Perpetual Wisdom in the Star-studded Canopy 15
   - 5.5. Venturing to the Cosmos 15
   - 5.6. Christianity in the Unfolding Universe 15
6. Bridging the Gap: Space Exploration and Theology 17
   - 6.1. Science and Theology: Foes or Allied Forces? 17

- 6.2. The Extraterrestrial Question: Revisit Theology ... 18
- 6.3. A Leap of Faith: Science and the Unknown ... 18
- 6.4. Jesus: A Universal Guidepost ... 19
- 6.5. Cosmic Spirituality: A Confluence ... 19
7. The Constellation of Beliefs: The Church and the Cosmos ... 20
    - 7.1. The Cosmos: From Geocentrism to Heliocentrism ... 20
    - 7.2. Christianity and Life Beyond Earth ... 21
    - 7.3. The Vatican Observatory ... 22
    - 7.4. Unifying Science and Spirituality ... 22
8. Scriptures and Stars: Biblical References to Extraterrestrials ... 24
    - 8.1. Extraterrestrial Life and The Bible: A Common Ground ... 24
    - 8.2. Celestial Entities: Angels and Beyond? ... 25
    - 8.3. The Heavenly Hosts: Other-worldly Civilizations? ... 25
    - 8.4. The Elohim and Cosmic Multiplicity ... 26
    - 8.5. The Biblical Cosmos: A Cosmic Mosaic? ... 26
9. Alien Life and Divine Design ... 28
    - 9.1. The Search for Extraterrestrial Life ... 28
    - 9.2. Divine Design and Life on Other Planets ... 29
    - 9.3. Extraterrestrial Life: Implication for Christian Faith ... 30
    - 9.4. Towards a Constructive Dialogue ... 30
10. The Missionary Aspect of Extraterrestrial Life ... 32
    - 10.1. The Calling Beyond Earth ... 32
    - 10.2. A New Perspective on The Great Commission ... 33
    - 10.3. Immaculate Imagination: Potential Forms of ET Life ... 33
    - 10.4. The Interstellar Church ... 34
11. Theological Implications of Alien Existence ... 35
    - 11.1. Delving into the Bible ... 35
    - 11.2. God's Infinite Creation ... 35
    - 11.3. Christ's Redemption and Extraterrestrial Life ... 36
    - 11.4. The Universality of Love ... 37

11.5. A Humble Humanity 37

Chapter 1. Introduction

Welcome to a remarkable and spirit-lifting journey through the cosmos with our special report, "Venturing Beyond Earth: Jesus and the Search for Extraterrestrial Life". This report intertwines a sense of spiritual quest with a fearless advent into the realm of scientific discovery, as it ventures into the vast universe in search of truths beyond our planet. We aim to reconcile faith with a quest onward to the stars, offering a fresh perspective on the larger questions of existence. This riveting and thought-provoking study holds a mirror up to two vastly different approaches to understanding our universe - through the teachings of Jesus and the relentless pursuit of science - with the hope of demonstrating that they might indeed be harmonious. This is an invigorating, and potentially transformative exploration that will leave you pondering the mysteries of the cosmos. Don't miss out on your chance to secure a copy of this limited-edition report!

Chapter 2. The Fusion of Faith and Science

Venturing into the realms of faith and science is, at its heart, a quest of understanding the human condition and the wider cosmos. These two pillars of thought have frequently found themselves at different crossroads, but through exploring the depth of each, we hope to find fascinating and harmonizing synergies between the two.

2.1. Understanding The Cosmos Through Science

Modern science has come a long way in unraveling mysteries of the universe that were long thought to be beyond human comprehension. Space exploration, predominantly shouldered by astrophysics, has identified endless galaxies, exotic celestial structures, and even hints of potential extraterrestrial life. Philosophers have pondered for ages: are we alone in the universe? Probing the cosmos allows science to inch closer to answering this age-old question.

Arguably, the vast universe might seem void and lifeless from our Earth-based perspective. Yet, the same laws of nature that govern our home planet apply across the cosmos, paving the way for a plethora of intriguing prospects. By understanding natural processes such as the formation of stars, galaxies, and planets, and exploring the possibility of other habitable environments, we are gradually bridging the gaps in our knowledge.

Through scientific advancements, mankind has sent several space missions, peering into distant corners of space, and detecting cosmic structures billions of light-years away. These explorations have fostered a sense of unity with the universe. As Apollo astronaut

Edgar Mitchell once stated, "Suddenly, from behind the rim of the Moon, in long, slow-motion moments of immense majesty, there it was rising... a sparkling blue and white delight."

2.2. Unfolding Jesus' Teachings

Parallel to the scientific zeal for cosmos study, we find the spiritual reflections upon life, purpose, and existence that find a cornerstone in the teachings of Jesus. Predominantly captured within the New Testament, the essence of these teachings offers a starkly contrasting, yet potentially harmonizing viewpoint.

Jesus' teachings encompass key aspects including love, compassion, forgiveness, and unity. They encourage belief in a benevolent divine force guiding all of existence - an omnipresent, omniscient, and omnipotent power, termed God, holding the cosmos together through love. The Bible (John 1:3) mentions, "Through him all things were made; without him nothing was made that has been made." This implies a profound interconnectedness among all creations, resonating the unity experienced by astronauts while viewing Earth from space.

An important facet of Jesus' philosophy also lies in the pursuit of truth, as he declared, "You will know the truth, and the truth will set you free" (John 8:32). Herein lies the potential crucible of fusion between faith and scientific exploration.

2.3. The Confluence of Faith and Science

The crossroads where faith and science meet is a fascinating territory. They might appear to be at odds, mostly due to their inherent approaches – faith born out of belief and spirituality, versus science, carved by skepticism and empirical evidence. Yet, the premise for both, albeit different in their means, is the same: to understand the cosmos and our place within it.

The nature of science is to question everything, to unravel how the world works, and to seek evidence for every claim. Contrastingly, faith, as mentioned in Hebrews 11:1, is "confidence in what we hope for and assurance about what we do not see." Bridging these two premises requires a subtle and delicate understanding.

Science is certainly an excellent tool for discovery. The extraterrestrial life that we seek and the exploration we undertake allows an empirical approach toward understanding the cosmos. Meanwhile, faith and the teachings of Jesus apply a similar pursuit toward comprehending the seemingly unseen aspects of reality - moral ideals, love, compassion, unity, and harmony.

2.4. Archway To Harmony

Historically, there have been instances where science and faith haven't seen eye to eye, born primarily from distinct interpretations of cosmic origins, among other things. Yet, at the same time, a vast number of scientists found their pursuits to be a form of 'spiritual' endeavour. Albert Einstein famously observed, "Science without religion is lame, religion without science is blind."

The quest for extraterrestrial life, interestingly, can be a rallying point for this synergy. The teachings of Jesus promote a universal love, void of alienation. It isn't a far stretch to apply such precepts to potential extraterrestrial beings. The scientific pursuit of finding such life pulses with the same frequency as the love and inclusivity embodied in Jesus's teachings.

Moreover, the awe-inspiring awe that the cosmos instills and the humbling realization of our tiny existence within it is a profound spiritual experience in itself - comparable to religious experiences. When we shift our perspective and approach these two distinct paths not as opposing, but complementary methodologies, the fusion of faith and science becomes not merely feasible but inherently existing.

Pioneering physicist and theologian John Polkinghorne once said, "The question of the existence of God is the single most important question we face about the nature of reality" - a question that interlaces scientific and spiritual exploration.

In conclusion, it's evident that faith and science need not be seen as competing domains, but rather as different lenses through which to view our exciting journey through the cosmos. As we continue this quest, unravelling more mysteries, there's a vast potential for faith and science to augment each other's strides in understanding this magnificent universe we share.

Chapter 3. Jesus's Teachings: A New Interpretation

In the light of our evolving understanding of the cosmos, Christians worldwide are reevaluating the interpretations of Jesus's teachings to reflect the possibility of extraterrestrial existence. The infinite majesty of space and the intricate wonder of potential alien life forms calls us to broaden our perspective and pushes our theology to be more cosmic and universal. Compelled by the scientific discoveries and clues suggested by modern astronomy, we dig deeper into the teachings of Jesus.

3.1. Jesus's Teachings and the Universe

Jesus often used parables to explain profound truths. These symbolic narratives, laden with deep meanings, can advance our understanding of the cosmos when reexamined in the context of our expanding universe.

The overarching theme noted in Jesus's parables, such as the Good Shepherd and Prodigal Son, is the boundless love and unending mercy of God, welcome to all. This narrative of an omnipresent, inclusive God invites humans to comprehend a God not limited by our earth, but instead operates in the entirety of the cosmos. If we view these illustrations as extending beyond our planet and encompassing extraterrestrial life, we open ourselves to a broader, more extensive comprehension of divine love and mercy.

The messages of kindness, selflessness, and compassion central to Jesus's teachings are universal truths human existence rests on, and presumably so would the existence of other intelligent forms of life. Strengthening these virtues amidst the anticipation of encountering extraterrestrial forms will foster universal peace and unity, aligning entirely with Jesus's teachings.

3.2. The Kingdom of God: An Expanded View

The 'Kingdom of God,' as Jesus described, was not of this world. This metaphorical kingdom, aimed at conveying God's rule over the hearts and minds of people, could be viewed as extending beyond merely Earthly bounds. It may well be a cosmic kingdom, including life throughout the universe.

Contemplating the Kingdom of God in a cosmic perspective imparts a sense of shared destiny among all life forms across the universe. It fosters a heightened empathy and sense of solidarity, breaking free from geographical borders and extending on an infinite, cosmic plane.

3.3. Jesus and Our Cosmic Neighbors

Jesus's teachings revolve around the attainment of unity and harmony. They celebrate diversity and teach acceptance. Ethics, empathy, and love form the basis of this philosophy, which aligns itself seamlessly with the idea of a multiverse teeming with different forms of life.

Imbuing these teachings into our interactions with potential extraterrestrial existence encourages constructive dialogue and peaceful co-existence, a testament to our evolved understanding of Jesus's lessons.

3.4. Concluding Thoughts

Reinterpreting Jesus's teachings through a universal lens prepares us for our future cosmic explorations. It softens dogmatic rigidity, allowing us to embrace new, wondrous possibilities.

Jesus encouraged us to seek truth and wisdom. Today, as we turn our gaze to the stars, we carry this spiritual quest alongside our scientific explorations, learning and growing as we progress. We embark upon an exciting, spirit-uplifting journey through Jesus's teachings and the cosmos, awaiting the grandeur of truths that lie beyond our planet.

Chapter 4. The Understanding of Life Beyond Earth

In the vast reaches of the cosmos, we humans have long sought answers to a primordial question: Are we alone? The quest for extraterrestrial life remains a crucial cornerstone of our space exploration programs, a search that blends modern science with enduring spiritual inquiries into the nature of our existence. But what might life beyond Earth truly mean, as seen through the lens of Christianity and other faiths, and how might it coexist with our scientific understanding of the universe?

4.1. Jesus: The Extraterrestrial Life and Christianity

The Christian faith's interpretation of Jesus Christ's teaching provides a fascinating entry point to this discourse. In John 10:16, Jesus mentions, "I have other sheep, that are not of this sheep pen. I must bring them also. They too will listen to my voice, and there shall be one flock, one shepherd." This humble phrase suggests a broader perspective, hinting at the existence of beings akin to humans but existing beyond our earthly realm, thus opening a spiritual window to the possibility of extraterrestrial life.

In this context, extraterrestrial beings, if they share our desire for truth, for divine love, could indeed be seen as part of Christ's unmentioned "sheep." This perspective allows us to reconcile the teachings of Jesus with the seemingly boundless variety of life we might find in the cosmos. The unification of these beliefs underlies the premise that God's reach extends across the universe, not merely limited to Earth.

4.2. Exploring the Unknown: Science at the Frontier

On the scientific front, the search for life beyond Earth is a tantalizing pursuit, fueled by advancements in astrobiology, planetary science, and space technology. The principal foundation lies in the Kepler's laws of planetary motion and the Copernican Principle, which suggests that Earth is not uniquely positioned in the universe. Under the light of these foundational theories, we understand that other stars, similar to our Sun, could harbor planets with the right conditions for life.

As we dive deeper into this cosmos, we find intriguing hints at the potential for life. From the rocky exoplanets twirling in the habitable zones of distant stars to the mysterious oceans beneath the icy shells of Jupiter's moon Europa and Saturn's moon Enceladus, prospects exist in abundance. Current and future endeavours like the James Webb Space Telescope will enable us to study distant worlds in unprecedented detail, possibly unearthing signs of biological activity, termed 'biosignatures.'

4.3. The Confluence: Where Spiritual Quest Meets Scientific Venture

While scriptures and science may seem to travel parallel paths, a point of convergence surfaces when we consider purpose. If we, as humans, are on a spiritual quest, that innate curiosity driving us toward the heavens might be seen as part of our divine make-up.

Scientists, in pursuit of extraterrestrial life, aim to understand the overarching evolutionary processes that govern life in the universe, a motivation not far-removed from religious adherents seeking to comprehend their place in the divine plan. The two approaches may differ in method, but they echo a shared sentiment: the quest to know and understand our universe's grand tapestry.

4.4. Working Hypotheses and Theology

It remains vital to emphasize that the existence of extraterrestrial life remains a working hypothesis in science, given the lack of direct evidence. A similar humble approach could apply to theological discussions on this topic. As we navigate this uncharted territory, openness to new discoveries and adaptability should guide us, while preserving an atmosphere of respect for diverse viewpoints.

4.5. Ethical Considerations on Extraterrestrial Life

Unraveling the mysteries of extraterrestrial life can present profound ethical implications, particularly in how we treat other life forms. This calls for the application of universal ethics, a principle central to the teachings of Jesus, who advocated compassion and kindness towards all. The golden rule of "do unto others as you would have them do unto you" finds clear relevance here, suggesting a universal guideline for our interactions beyond Earth.

4.6. Conclusion: A Conscious Leap Into the Vast Cosmos

As we blend Christian theology with space exploration, we find a unique and compelling perspective on life beyond Earth. The spiritual quest for purpose and the scientific exploration for understanding can indeed coexist harmoniously, together weaving a rich tapestry of knowledge and sensibility. This interplay between theology and science not only ushers in a profound sense of kinship with potential cosmic neighbors but also fosters evolution towards a more inclusive and open-minded society.

In the end, our journey towards understanding life beyond Earth becomes more than a scientific endeavor. It transforms into a grand celestial voyage of spiritual self-discovery, a recognition of our place in the cosmos, and the realization that we are, as Carl Sagan so succinctly put it, "Starstuff, contemplating the stars."

Investigating the intersection of faith and the quest for extraterrestrial life offers us a rich ground for self-reflection, a challenge, and an opportunity to expand our sense of self, of community, and possibly, of divinity. As we send our probes and craft into the vast cosmos, we embark on a journey of exploration that is as much inward as it is upward. In this exploration, there is the potential for a profound meeting of the mind and spirit, each informing the other in a continual dance of discovery and understanding.

Chapter 5. Christianity in the Era of Astronomical Discoveries

In the blink of an eye, a single flash of divine inspiration led to the explosion of development in the arena of celestial knowledge. The ancient astronomers saw the night sky as a celestial theatre, where the magnificence of the Creator could be seen. With every new discovery, humanity developed increasingly advanced comprehension about the enormity of the cosmos. Let's embark on a remarkable journey escorting science and religion through the annals of Christianity's encounter with astronomical discoveries.

5.1. The Astronomical Pursuit in the Middle Ages

The Christian Middle Ages were a fertile ground for the budding study of astronomy. While popular philosophy often categorized this era as a 'Dark Age' for scientific inquiry, it formed the cornerstone for the later explosion of astronomical understanding. Monasteries and religious institutions served as the bedrocks of literacy, knowledge preservation, and scientific investigation.

The Venerable Bede, an English monk during the 7th-century, authored the notable work 'The Reckoning of Time,' providing comprehensive instruction on the movement of celestial bodies, including an introduction to computing the date of Easter. His work represented Christianity's alignment with the broader quest for understanding the cosmos as God's creation, not as an object of worship itself but as a mirror reflecting divine wonder.

5.2. Towards Enlightened Horizons

The 16th-century marked a significant shift in Christian engagement with astronomy as Nicolaus Copernicus proposed the heliocentric model, replacing Ptolemy's earth-centered universe which had been accepted by the Church for over a millennium. Despite emerging opposition, dedicated luminaries like Johannes Kepler and Galileo Galilei advanced Copernican insights, laying fundamental principles of astronomy in motion and inertia.

While Galileo's struggles with Church authorities over heliocentrism might seem to suggest a rift between science and faith, historical reading shows that their dispute was largely founded on methodological and interpretative misunderstandings. Contrary to frequent portrayal, the Church did not despise reason or science. Rather, it celebrated them as gifts from God to uncover the enigma of the cosmos. In a letter to the Grand Duchess Christina, Galileo himself wrote that interpretation of the Bible, when it appears to conflict with scientific evidence, requires prudent contemplation as Scripture and Creation, both works of God, cannot be in contradiction.

5.3. Design in the Great Clockwork Universe

The 17th-century gave birth to Isaac Newton's monumental laws of motion and universal gravitation. The universe was likened to a giant clockwork mechanism, set in motion by the Creator. Newton believed that his scientific work was a mode of worship, a way to understand and appreciate the divine laws governing God's universe.

Studying the night sky was the erudite's religious duty, as it embodied the glory of a 'Divine Craftsman.' There was no dichotomy between scientific observations and faith as the intricate laws bearing testament to divine design served to enhance their awe of the Creator.

5.4. Perpetual Wisdom in the Star-studded Canopy

Understanding of our universe continued to expand with scientific advancements. In the face of growing secularism during the 18th and 19th centuries, the Church navigated a new relationship with science.

A reassertion of design arguments took place, asserting that the complexity and beauty of the physical universe pointed toward a Creator's hand. William Paley's watchmaker analogy in his work 'Natural Theology' suggested that just like a watch hints at a watchmaker, the precision and arrangement of the universe reveal a Designer.

5.5. Venturing to the Cosmos

The 20th-century heralded unprecedented strides in space exploration. The Vatican established its own astronomical research institute - the Vatican Observatory - to demonstrate that the Church is not against scientific progress but more than willing to engage with the truths uncovered by scientific inquiry. Pope Pius XII, in his 1950 encyclical Humani Generis, confirmed that the Church does not oppose the theory of evolution. Rather, scientific theories should be explored as long as God's role as the originator of all life is affirmed.

5.6. Christianity in the Unfolding Universe

Even the most recent astronomical discoveries can coexist with Christian faith. Intriguing observations about our universe, whether it be the existence of exoplanets capable of hosting life, the enigma of dark matter and dark energy, or the profound implications of a multiverse - all serve to broaden the canvas on which we perceive God's creation. In this view, Archbishop James Ussher's 17th-century claim of Earth's creation on October 23, 4004 BC, becomes a rather limited interpretation.

Uncovering the magnitude and complexities of the cosmos doesn't distance believers from Christianity. Instead, discoveries become a humbling reminder of our small place in the grand design and the infinite fascination and brilliance of our Creator.#+END

Enduring through centuries, Christianity has interpreted and weaved astronomical knowledge into its fabric of faith. Astronomical discoveries have consistently echoed the sentiment of Psalm 19:1, "The heavens declare the glory of God; the skies proclaim the work of his hands." This signifies that an exploration of the cosmos complements the journey of faith, fostering a deeper reflection of God's immense creative power and persistent love.

Chapter 6. Bridging the Gap: Space Exploration and Theology

Astounding as it may seem, our human minds, in their ceaseless quest for understanding, have carved out domains of knowledge that sometimes appear to be at odds with one another. Uncompromisingly, space exploration - a marvelous product of scientific enlightenment - and theology - quintessentially spiritual and profound - often seem like two different worlds. However, to venture beyond our terrestrial confines and explore the mysteries cosmos, we would do well to reconcile these two.

6.1. Science and Theology: Foes or Allied Forces?

Not so long ago, questions of existence were ranged under the domain of religious scholars. With the advent of the scientific revolution, however, this scenario changed. Science took over the exploration of the natural world, and with time, the spiritual seemed to recede into the shadows.

The discord isn't surprising. After all, the tools of examination in science - evidence, experimentation, and empirical truth - may appear to be sharply contrasting with the axioms of faith that demand acceptance. And yet, is it really so?

Perhaps not. As we cast our gaze upon the vast and unfolding universe through telescopes and probes, we do not merely seek to answer questions about star formations, black holes, and alien life; we are essentially making a spiritual quest too. We're seeking answers about ourselves, our origin, and our place in the grand design of things – are these not fundamentally questions of our spirit?

6.2. The Extraterrestrial Question: Revisit Theology

The prospect of extraterrestrial life forms invites us to revisit our theological perspectives. While no religious scripture specifically mentions aliens, it's important to consider the overarching themes of understanding and universal love present in the teachings of Jesus. If God's love extends to all His creation, should it not also include beings from beyond our Earth?

In the Gospel of John, Jesus says, "In my Father's house are many rooms" (John 14:2). Could these 'rooms' also hold a place for our extra-terrestrial neighbors? While the fundamental teachings of Jesus do not provide specific details about life beyond Earth, they do provide a framework that allows for an expansion of theological understanding and acceptance of the unknown.

6.3. A Leap of Faith: Science and the Unknown

It's important to understand that despite its empirical foundations, science often requires a leap of faith. For example, the acceptance of the Big Bang theory – the sudden and violent explosion from a singularity that supposedly kick-started our universe – necessitates faith in scientific discoveries and deductions made by cosmologists.

In essence, the scientist must trust the data and the instruments that led to the creation of the theory, much in the same way that believers trust in the holy scriptures and their interpretations. The apparent rift between science and theology in understanding the universe, is, therefore, not as wide as it may appear at first.

6.4. Jesus: A Universal Guidepost

For believers, Jesus is a moral and spiritual guidepost. His teachings echo the basic human principles of kindness, love, understanding, and justice. While these teachings come from a terrestrial perspective, they hold universal value.

Even as we embark on this exciting search for extraterrestrial life, these values can guide us. For the prospect of a new form of life should not incite fear and hostility, but a desire to understand, love and accept, as Jesus taught us to do.

6.5. Cosmic Spirituality: A Confluence

As we set forth on the quest beyond our planetary home, we're not just taking a scientific journey but a spiritual one too. The awe and wonder that the universe inspires intimates at a form of Cosmic Spirituality, a confluence of scientific curiosity and religious wonder.

This meeting point, where science and religion can coexist and inform each other, will be key to our understanding and explorations of the mysteries of the universe. The shared intellectual humility required by both scientific and theological enquiry may eventually spawn a more encompassing perspective of our cosmic home.

Our voyage across the cosmos thus presents a unique opportunity: to bridge the seemingly vast gap between theology and science, to build friendships across philosophical lines, and to encourage an integrated outlook that embraces both scientific curiosity and spiritual aspiration. After all, aren't we all, in our own ways, reaching for the stars?

Chapter 7. The Constellation of Beliefs: The Church and the Cosmos

Established traditions cast long, sturdy roots, firmly instilled in the minds of those who heed them. Religion, in particular Christianity, is one such tradition that has permeated civilization's collective consciousness, guiding moral and ethical frameworks, whilst influencing our understanding of the universe indirectly. The Church, a fundamental institution of faith, has had a significant relationship with humanity's perception of the cosmos. This intricate interlacing, at times harmonious and other times contentious, forms the focus of our exploration, as we delve into the Church's perspective of the universe and its place within it.

7.1. The Cosmos: From Geocentrism to Heliocentrism

Historically, the Church embraced geocentrism - the belief that the Earth stood at the center of the universe, with the rest of the celestial bodies moving concentrically around it. This geocentrism found its foundations in biblical interpretations and was fortified by early Greek philosophies, particularly those embarked upon by Aristotle and Ptolemy.

However, the dawn of the Renaissance and the progression of scientific thought challenged this view. Nicolaus Copernicus, a clergyman himself, presented an alternative, revolutionary model: heliocentrism. His work 'On the Revolutions of the Celestial Spheres' stipulated that the sun, not Earth, was the center of the universe. Although controversial, over the years, with contributions from astronomers such as Kepler and Galileo, heliocentrism received increasing acceptance.

The Church was, however, initially reluctant to embrace this shift in paradigm. The trial of Galileo Galilei, a firm promoter of heliocentrism, marked a critical point in the Church's history-influencing cosmic thought. Though Galileo's house arrest was more due to his perceived arrogance and irreverence rather than strictly his scientific views, it is seen by many as a symbol of the Church's opposition to scientific progress.

Over time, this perception has changed. Maciej Szczepanski, a church historian, wrote, "The current stance of the Catholic Church is one of accepting scientific models as providing valuable data about physical processes. But this does not constrain the Church's teachings on a spiritual level."

7.2. Christianity and Life Beyond Earth

As voyages beyond our planet edge further into science fiction's realm, the Church is engaging with these developments, fostering dialogues around extraterrestrial existence. It attempts to reconcile these discoveries whilst adhering to biblical foundations - an intricate task, indeed.

The central query revolves around the idea of salvation. Can extraterrestrial beings receive salvation as per the teachings of Jesus? Many church leaders suggest that their acceptance of such a possibility would not threaten their theology significantly. They argue that the central tenets of Christianity - love, humility, and charity - would hold, irrespective of other-worldly beings.

The late Monsignor Corrado Balducci, a Catholic theologian of the Vatican Curia, a close friend to Pope St. John Paul II, once stated, "Extra-terrestrial life does not contradict our faith."

7.3. The Vatican Observatory

The Vatican remains an active player in astronomical research; it maintains an Observatory and runs summer schools for young astronomers. The Observatory represents a significant step in the Church's attempt to reconcile its beliefs with a continually shifting conception of the cosmos.

Its team of Jesuit brothers and priests conduct cutting-edge research across various arenas of astronomy and astrophysics, representing the Church's active engagement with scientific advancement. Notably, the current Director, Brother Guy Consolmagno, even co-authored a book entitled "Would You Baptize an Extraterrestrial?" indicating the intersection of faith and science in the Church's discourse.

7.4. Unifying Science and Spirituality

Presently, the Church does not view science as a threat but as a tool to understand God's creation better. It insists that the perceived conflict between science and religion arises primarily from a misunderstanding of their respective domains. The Church sees science and faith as complementary, rather than competitive.

Saint John Paul II famously said, "Science can purify religion from error and superstition. Religion can purify science from idolatry and false absolutes."

This reconciliation of belief systems continues to be an ongoing process. There is an increasing willingness within the Church to engage with scientific advancements, reflected by a stronger emphasis on the intersection of faith and reason.

Exploring these perspectives, the Church's approach has largely evolved from defending the fortress of religion against the perceived onslaught of science. Today, it attempts to unite these seemingly disparate entities, embodying a spirit of embracing shared truths and dialogue. This journey speaks volumes about our human endeavor to expand our understanding and foster unity in this vast, diverse universal expanse.

In the grand spectacle of the cosmos, the Church stands as a bastion of beliefs navigating the sea of scientific advancement. Recognizing the consilience in the teachings of Jesus and the unfolding truths of the cosmos offers a broader, more inclusive perspective on existence, marking a significant stride in humanity's eternal quest for knowledge. After all, every starlight in the cosmos is a beckon, a call for exploration - not just of distant celestial bodies, but of the dimensions within our own beings, and the deepest enigmas of faith.

Chapter 8. Scriptures and Stars: Biblical References to Extraterrestrials

The Bible transcends ages as a sacred text revered by billions worldwide. Though its primary domain is spiritual, moral, and existential concerns, various interpretations permit leaning towards a cosmological perspective. In our endeavor for extraterrestrial discovery, it's pertinent to first chart down these scholarly interpretations of several biblical Scriptures.

8.1. Extraterrestrial Life and The Bible: A Common Ground

One might wonder: Does the Bible reference extraterrestrial life? The answer isn't straightforward. While the biblical text does not categorically refer to or dismiss non-earthly life, certain verses yield tantalizing interpretations when viewed from the perspective of cosmic life.

A prime example is found in the Gospel of John (John 10:16), where Jesus says: "I have other sheep that are not of this sheep pen. I must bring them also. They too will listen to my voice, and there shall be one flock and one shepherd." The term "other sheep" could be seen as allegorical, symbolizing individuals or people outside of His immediate followers. Yet some interpreters have speculated these 'other sheep' may refer to intelligent life beyond our world. Jesus' mission was universal, and if life does exist elsewhere, God's love and provisions could logically extend to them.

8.2. Celestial Entities: Angels and Beyond?

We frequently encounter 'heavenly beings' in the Scriptures - angels, predominantly. They are described as entities originating outside our realm. Could these celestial beings be deemed extraterrestrial or multidimensional life forms as perceived in our modern understanding?

As portrayed in the Bible, angels are not bound by earthly physics or biology. They appear to move between dimensions (Heaven and Earth) and manipulate physical matter. This has led to a thought-provoking hypothesis that, in the light of modern science, these beings could be entities from other dimensions or parts of the universe. This speculative line of thought, however, is held by a small minority within the scientific and religious community.

8.3. The Heavenly Hosts: Other-worldly Civilizations?

The Bible makes frequent references to 'heavenly hosts'. In most contexts, this term is understood as armies of angels or spiritual beings. But what if we took 'heavenly' to mean 'cosmic'? Could the referents here be advanced civilizations beyond our planet?

Ancient cultures were known to refer to celestial bodies allegorically. The ancients used terminologies that were the best match to their times and contexts. Modern interpretations propose that the 'heavenly hosts' could be civilizations from distant galaxies or planets.

While such an exploration might seem an enormous stretch to traditional theology, it invites curiosity about our understanding of the universe and God's creation, encouraging dialogue between faith and scientific discovery.

8.4. The Elohim and Cosmic Multiplicity

The Hebrew Bible (Old Testament) introduces the term 'Elohim' - a plural form generally used to denote God. This plural grammatical form has sparked numerous debates among scholars and theologians. Some maintain it's merely a traditional language style, but others argue it may suggest a multiplicity of divine entities.

In the cosmological context, could 'Elohim' imply a pantheon of cosmic beings or advanced civilizations? Admittedly, this interpretation is unorthodox. Yet if we examine the language and metaphors used within their historical context (where plural forms didn't just denote respect but also multiplicity), the suggestion becomes less extraneous.

8.5. The Biblical Cosmos: A Cosmic Mosaic?

The biblical proportion of the cosmos, as described in the Scriptures, is a vast augmentation from our Earth-bound perspective. The Bible speaks of the existence of the 'heavens' and 'many dwelling places' in God's realm.

For example, in John 14:2 (NIV), Jesus states: "In my Father's house are many rooms. If that were not so, would I have told you that I am going there to prepare a place for you?" This has traditionally been interpreted as an assurance of an afterlife for believers. Modern interpretations, within the cosmic perspective, suggest these may refer to distant worlds or civilizations in the cosmic expanse.

Dissecting these verses from a cosmic perspective doesn't dispel their spiritual significance. Instead, these interpretations can herald a broader understanding of God's creation, inviting scientists and believers alike to explore the cosmos with awe and reverence.

While our venture into the stars can spark new interpretations, it's crucial that we approach these with humility and respect for the original texts. These hypotheses of biblical 'extraterrestrial' references aren't definitive but can enhance our probing for cosmic truths and the divine.

Biblical Scriptures are informed by rich and abstract metaphorical language that allows for a broad range of interpretations. Just as earthly life reflects the divine in manifold forms, we might consider that the cosmic canvas may also be teeming with life, each stroke an expression of God's infinite creativity.

In sum, the Bible isn't a scientific handbook, but when observed through the lens of modern cosmology, it presents thought-provoking passages that can be sculpted into building blocks for harmonizing faith and science.

Chapter 9. Alien Life and Divine Design

Since antiquity, humans have looked into the endless night's sky, insatiably curious about the potential existence of life beyond our terrestrial boundaries. The scientific quest for extraterrestrial life and the Christian teachings of divine design seem to be two distinct spheres of thought, yet they share a common thread - the quest for understanding the nature and origins of life in the universe that we inhabit. This exploration into alien life and the divine design aims to delve into those profound questions and seek common ground between science and faith.

9.1. The Search for Extraterrestrial Life

The scientific journey towards discovering extraterrestrial life has been rife with a dynamic interplay of astounding discoveries and resounding silence. The vast universe filled with numerous galaxies, each with countless stars and orbiting planets, hints at the high probability of life beyond our planet.

Our advancements in technology have powered this expedition, from Robert Hooke's first glimpses of Mars through his telescope in the 17th century to the launching of robotic spacecrafts like Voyager and Mars Rover. These missions have provided us with valuable information, including the discovery of water in Mars's poles, possible traces of life in the Venusian atmosphere, and potentially habitable exoplanets in the Goldilocks zones around their stars.

The field of astrobiology has expanded remarkably, building mathematical models for estimating the likelihood of life, such as the Drake Equation. This seminal equation considers factors such as the rate of star formation, the fraction of stars with planetary systems, the number of Earth-like planets per system, and the plausible lifespan of a communicative civilization.

Despite these calculated probabilities and promising discoveries, a definitive evidence of extraterrestrial life remains elusive. This gaping silence in our search, often known as the Fermi Paradox, could be because life might not be as common as we think, or the technological civilizations might invariably destroy themselves. Alternatively, we might not be looking in the right places or not be capable of comprehending or detecting the signs of alien life yet.

9.2. Divine Design and Life on Other Planets

Christian teachings and scriptural interpretations don't explicitly address alien life. However, the belief in divine design guides us to a possible understanding in this matter. The Bible emphasizes God's creative power and omnipotence, suggesting that the creation of life elsewhere Does not conflict with these fundamental beliefs.

In Genesis 1:1, it states, "In the beginning God created the heavens and the earth," not limiting God's creation to the Earth alone. Furthermore, in John 1:3 it's noted "Through him all things were made; without him nothing was made that has been made." The premise stated here is not exclusively earthly, indicating that if God chose to create life elsewhere, it is within His divine prerogative.

God's design is often seen as an explanation for the sublime complexities and nuances of life on Earth, from the delicate balance of nature to the intricate workings of cells. Hence the discovery of extraterrestrial life could be viewed as a testament to God's boundless creativity and design.

9.3. Extraterrestrial Life: Implication for Christian Faith

The discovery of life elsewhere would undeniably have profound theological implications. It raises questions on the unique role and importance of humans in creation, original sin, Jesus Christ's salvation, and other Christian beliefs. Should we believe that other life forms share in God's plan for salvation, or are we fundamentally unique?

In the Bible, humans are considered God's special creation, imprinted with his image, making us a unique part of the divine scheme. Discovering intelligent alien life could challenge this belief, but it could also broaden our perspective on God's creation.

As for salvation, Jesus Christ's incarnation, crucifixion, and resurrection are the cornerstone of Christian faith. Assuming alien civilizations exist, one could wonder if they are sinless or, like us, require salvation. If so, have they had their own Savior, or does Christ's salvation extend to all sentient beings across the cosmos? It is possible that the divine plan might play out differently across different worlds, yet remain within the bounds of God's infinite wisdom and mercy.

9.4. Towards a Constructive Dialogue

Far from being irreconcilable, the pursuits of science and faith can have a constructive dialogue at the intersection of the search for extraterrestrial life and divine design. Science continues its search, bringing back results in bits and spurts, pushing the frontiers of our knowledge. Faith, on the other hand, serves as a moral compass and a source of spiritual comfort, illuminating human existence's grander questions with eternal truths.

The exploration of the cosmos prompts the reevaluation and enrichment of our understanding of God's creation, encouraging an evolving faith that can assimilate new discoveries into its theological framework. Engaging with these questions brings us closer to an understanding of ourselves as part of a larger cosmos, perhaps alongside other God-created beings, unified in our search for purpose and meaning.

The ongoing quest for extraterrestrial life, through the lenses of both scientific exploration and faith-based introspection, can be an exhilarating journey towards an advanced comprehension of life, the universe, and humanity's place within it.

This exploration into alien life and divine design is not an exercise for resolution, but a drive to plumb the depths of our collective curiosity. The curtain remains only slightly raised on the stage of cosmic exploration, beckoning us to keep seeking and keep wondering, for both science and faith are part of this grand cosmic narrative. Through the scientific method's rigor and the light of spirituality, we might journey beyond the known edges and find a deeper understanding of our place in the universe.

Chapter 10. The Missionary Aspect of Extraterrestrial Life

From the time humans first recognized the stars in the skies as distant suns, we've felt a pull towards them, their mysteries compelling us on a quest spanning millennia. In Christian context, a similar pull has been experienced—the call to share the teachings of Jesus, with love and understanding, to all corners of the Earth.

The notion of missionaries traveling beyond our planet into extraterrestrial realms aligns the Christian duty of spreading the Gospel with our interstellar curiosity. What could be a more profound testament to God's limitless love and the reach of Jesus' teachings than a quest that promises to extend across galaxies, possibly leading to encounters with civilization unknown to humanity?

10.1. The Calling Beyond Earth

Mark 16:15 reads, "And he said to them, 'Go into all the world and proclaim the Gospel to the whole creation.'" Could it be, then, that 'the whole of creation' includes not only our planet but all potentially life-sustaining worlds graced by the universal touch of the Creator? With the discovery of exoplanets, the idea has gained more ground, suggesting potential for life—unseen, unstudied, underappreciated in its potential-diversity—that waits to hear God's word.

Yet, it is essential to proceed with thoughtfulness. Communicating the Gospel's message requires understanding the recipient's receptivity, willing or otherwise. It presupposes human-like consciousness, the capacity to comprehend religious concepts, and a framework within which such ideas might make sense. Yet, are we to deny the Gospel to intelligent life forms from alien worlds merely because they might comprehend existence differently?

10.2. A New Perspective on The Great Commission

These questions necessitate a broader interpretation of The Great Commission. It may invite thinking beyond human paradigms of understanding, transcending the apparent barriers of thought and cognition. We presume that God's capacity to impart understanding is boundless, requiring us to be astute explorers and communicators, able to share Jesus' teachings in ways that resonate with diverse intelligent life forms.

On one hand, this requires scientific rigor, understanding the biology, psychology, and potential modes of communication of extraterrestrial life, thereby ensuring the message's safe transit across an astronomical cultural divide. On the other hand, it necessitates a spiritual openness, a readiness to appreciate 'otherness' and to share the richness of the Gospel's message with beings beyond our comprehension.

10.3. Immaculate Imagination: Potential Forms of ET Life

The quest extends beyond seeking potential sentient life forms; We must also expand our ability to comprehend the possibility of such manifestations. Earth's biodiversity presents us with a model to extrapolate potential alien life forms. Could there be life forms that communicate through patterns of light, radio waves, or even ways our senses can't perceive? How can we account for such diversity in our sacred mission?

Christians are called upon to appreciate God's creation in its full spectrum, and the teachings of Jesus can be seen as a way to bridge the gulf between humans and alien species. If we can love our neighbors on Earth, who might be vastly different from us, we might be able to extend that love to our neighbors in the cosmos.

10.4. The Interstellar Church

Envision, then, an interstellar Church, extending its influence not only across geographical territories on Earth, but expanding its influence into the Cosmos. This Church would need to be both rooted in the unchanging Gospel and open to the changing universe, adapting its methods as necessary while keeping its message eternal.

The missionary aspect of extraterrestrial life, while challenging our mind's limits does not seek to dismantle long-held dogmas but rather expands them to encompass the full grandeur of God's creation. Guided by the spirit of exploration and driven by the benevolent intentions of spreading the message of Jesus, humanity might find itself on the precipice of a new ecclesiastical reality—one that truly spans the cosmos.

Extraterrestrial missionary work employs the most exceptional machinery of the cosmos—faith and science. The journey of faith prompts us to venture into the vast unknown with the message of the Gospel, and science guides our steps to reach there. This duality, while seeming contradictory, signifies two facets of the same coin—our desire to understand the universe and our place within it.

Thus, the missionary aspect of extraterrestrial life is more than an ambition—it's a tribute to God's creation, scientific curiosity, and our spiritual aspirations. As we gaze upon the heavens and take our humble first steps toward the interstellar Church, let us be guided by the teachings of Jesus and the marvels of science, unveiling the mysterium tremendum et fascinans — the tremendous and fascinating mystery — that is the universe.

Chapter 11. Theological Implications of Alien Existence

The excitement surrounding our venture beyond Earth keeps mounting as yet another satellite propels into the infinite expanse. As this journey progresses, the potential for immeasurable discoveries can't help but dominate our thoughts. In tandem with these scientific explorations, it's worthwhile to reflect on the theological implications of the possible discovery of extraterrestrial life. A convergence of faith and science offers a unique perspective to grapple with these mysteries that have since forever captivated and inspired us.

11.1. Delving into the Bible

Whether the existence of alien life contradicts or aligns with biblical teachings is a subject of fervent dialogue among theologians. Traditional theological perspectives are grounded in biblical texts, which make no explicit reference to extraterrestrial life. Yet, the scriptures also do not explicitly deny the existence of life beyond Earth.

Many argue that the Bible, written in a pre-scientific era, was likely to focus on the Earth and humans' relationship with God. The focus was on our existence within the limits of our human understanding and did not venture into space. However, the Bible's silence on extraterrestrial life is not irrefutable evidence of its non-existence from a theological point of view.

11.2. God's Infinite Creation

If one were to adhere to the belief that God created everything in the universe, then it would be remiss not to acknowledge the potential for other life forms in the cosmos. Infinite in His might and capacity, God's ability to create is not limited to our world. The Book of Genesis offers us a glimpse into this - "In the beginning God created the heavens and the earth." (Genesis 1:1). Thereby implying the creation of entities beyond our planet.

If alien life were discovered, it would affirm the Christian view of God as the creator of all, emphasizing His limitless creative power. Life beyond Earth is simply a testament to God's insurmountable creative prowess.

11.3. Christ's Redemption and Extraterrestrial Life

A crucial facet of Christian belief lies in the divine narrative of Jesus Christ's incarnation, crucifixion, and resurrection. This represents a paradigm of redemption and salvation for humanity. But would the existence of extraterrestrial life challenge this earth-centric redemption story?

The theologian Thomas O'Meara proposed the concept of "Multiple Incarnations" and argued that if God could become incarnate as a human being on Earth, God could also manifest Himself among other intelligent civilizations should they exist. This concept, though contentious, aims to reconcile the existence of extraterrestrial life with the sacred narrative of Christ's redemption.

Others, borrowing from C.S. Lewis' "Space Trilogy," argue for a 'Supralapsarian view.' Here, extraterrestrial life forms are seen to be sin-free, unaffected by humanity's Original Sin and may not require redemption. These perspectives might ask us to reconsider our understanding of sin and salvation.

11.4. The Universality of Love

Jesus teaches us to "Love your neighbor as yourself" (Mark 12:31), embodying the idea of immeasurable and boundless love. By contextualizing this message in an interstellar setting, our understanding of 'neighbor' extends beyond geographical and even planetary boundaries.

This love's universality could be applied to respect and care for any sentient life, extraterrestrial or otherwise. This perspective aligns with the Christian imperative of love, underlining the potential interconnectedness of us all, bound by the cosmic fabric of God's creation.

11.5. A Humble Humanity

The discovery of extraterrestrial life could potentially instigate a transformative shift in our human self-perception. We may need to relinquish our assumed superiority, acknowledging ourselves as a small part of a vastly diverse cosmos teeming with life.

This humility embodies Christian teachings of humbleness and might serve as a reminder of our dependence on God's grace, emphasizing "For by grace you have been saved through faith, not by works, so that no one can boast." (Ephesians 2:8-9)

The contemplation of theological implications surrounding alien existence can be mind-boggling. The lack of conclusive answers stimulates further exploration of this ethereal intersection of faith and science. It propounds us to remain open-minded, humble, and always willing to learn.

As we venture beyond Earth, reconciling faith with scientific quest becomes pertinent. Irrespective of the theological conclusions we might draw, the pursuit reflects our collective yearning for expansion and comprehension, spiritually and scientifically. This illustrates an innate curiosity which, in of itself, is a reflection of the divine curiosity that set the stars in motion. Christianity and science need not stand contrasted but rather be seen as different interpretations of the same cosmic narrative, ultimately leading us to Truth.

Printed by Amazon Italia Logistica S.r.l.
Torrazza Piemonte (TO), Italy